Blaq-Qaeda

The NBA as a terror cell

Blaq-Qaeda

The NBA as a terror cell

A Novel

By

Michael Shelly

ISBN 978-1-257-98913-3

ACT I

PROLOGUE

He walked out of the restaurant feelin' good, all 6 feet 11 inches of him feelin' real goddamn good. And more than a little wasted from all that fine-ass coke he'd sucked up. Hell yeah he was feelin' good! Not a problem in the fuckin' world! Just like his agent said, this was his time, this here and now, and he was gonna make damn sure he grabbed everything he could!

He was the man, and everyone who saw his bad black ass on the court knew it. Leading the league in scoring again, just like last year as a rookie. And sure as shit, long as he took care of his business on the court, all this fine-ass livin' would last, too.

Long as he could play ball it always be just like tonight, man, with waiters bowing down low to him and high class little white bitches circling his table like pretty little butterflies ready to suck his dick at the wink of an eye. And dealers, oh man, those righteous brothers, digging deep into their pockets to offer up free shit every time he got up to take a piss. What more could you want?

This had to be fuckin' heaven, man!

He was a rich nigger. A very rich nigger in a country that most definitely feared rich niggers. And that meant he could do 'bout anything he damn well pleased. Shit, all you had to do was ask O.J. 'bout that shit, right? Or at least until he pressed his luck and pulled that bonehead caper in Vegas. And that Stallworth cat, the brother that got so fucked up he couldn't see and then mowed down some worthless spick in Florida and got a whole of 30 days for wastin' the dude, proved it beyond any fuckin' doubt!

Man, rich niggers ruled America! From sea to shinin' sea!

Few years back, his pops wanted him to stay in school and get that bullshit degree, but, man, wasn't that jus' like any tired old Uncle Tom nigger playin' up to the white man! Could only take that school shit for a year. He needed respect, and money, and where he came from ya sure as shit didn't get any of that with no college. So he split for the big time. The fuckin' NBA, man. And instantly got all the respect money and fame could buy.

School? Fuck that shit. Bet your sweet black ass none of them prissy little white boys he went to school with ever owned a custom-made Mercedes like his. And paid for with cash, man, cash. Cool, cool cash. And most definitely bet your ass none of them had hot-assed women in every city crawlin' around on their knees and beggin' for him to slip them a little black dick every now and then like he did. No way any kind of book learnin' would have done any of that shit for him.

That thought suddenly made him stop and laugh.

Prissy little bookworms and nasty, big-titty whores! No way they would ever taste the life he had. And Lordy, Lordy, Lordy, what a sweet life it was! All the way from New York to L.A. and back again!

"Fuck no they won't," he mumbled and began slowly stumbling toward his car again, unaware of nothing but the cold black night around him.

As he walked and suddenly realized just how far away he'd parked, he wondered again why the hell he always ended up here at this shithole, 'specially when he knew good and goddamn well they didn't have no valet parking. And shit, man, any nigger leading the fuckin' National Basketball Association in scoring shouldn't have to walk his ass nowheres.

A familiar voice quickly brought him back from his thoughts.

"Damn dawg, ya leave any that fine white pussy for us?" the voice drawled as he and two others in baggy jeans and hoodies and with enough gold dangling from their necks to probably buy an NBA team got out of a silver Jag that had just pulled into the parking lot. The man coughed and passed a joint when they got closer.

"Y'all know how I love that tight white pussy, my man!"

"Shit, jus' tryin' to do what I can to help the poor white man take care of his bitches, ya' know!" the superstar laughed, sucking greedily on the joint and then grabbing his crotch and thrusting it forward several times.

"Ain't no one got a dick like a nigger, know what I'm sayin', man!"

"Ride on, nigger! the man drawled. "Ride fuckin' on. Cool game tonight, man. Real cool! Y'all kicked some ass!"

"Kickin' ass my thing, brother."

Taking one last deep drag before passing the joint back, he turned and began walking toward his car again.

"Peace out, my brothers," he yelled over his shoulder, then shot his arm up, fist clenched, in an old school salute.

Three other men in a dark sedan parked not far from where the Jag had pulled in watched him stop for a second to share a hit with the group from the Jag, do his Tommie Smith imitation and then continue on towards his black Mercedes in the rear of the nearly deserted parking lot. He was definitely feeling no pain. That was good. It was also good that he'd parked his pride and joy in an isolated, badly lit area, probably in an effort to spare the vehicle a few dings every now and then. But all it did tonight was make their job that much easier.

"Fuckin' nigger," the driver spat, shaking his head in disgust. "Bad ass superstar, huh,"

He added as a smile crossed his dark, unshaven face. "Not for much longer."

The man in the passenger seat, who looked as crisp as if he had just stepped out of a Marine Corp recruiting poster, merely nodded at his partner's chatter and his nervous tapping on the steering wheel. He'd worked with him many times in the past and knew it was just his way of blowing off a little steam until their moment came. The third man in the back seat remained silent, seemingly brooding over something, his eyes never leaving the man weaving towards his car.

The two in the front had gone over their target's file a thousand times. They knew his habits, as well as his disgusting sexual preferences, backwards and forwards. He frequented this one particular run-down restaurant in Hollywood whenever his team was in town. A joint reeking of sex, dealers, pimps and whores and anything else that satisfied one's wants and needs and all under one roof like a regular Wal-Mart. So it was pretty much expected for him to leave right before closing time so satisfied and stoned that he couldn't pay much attention to anything other than just putting one size 19 foot in front of the other when he staggered through the dark deserted parking lot. Being suspicious of anyone or anything wasn't on his mind.

The man finally reached his car and slumped by the door, fumbling inside his coat pocket for the keys. Head down and mumbling to himself, he never saw the two men exit the sedan parked only twenty feet away. They approached quickly.

"Excuse me…" the marine look-a-like announced in a soft, polite voice as they reached him. He too was reaching under his coat as he spoke.

The basketball player turned around unsteadily, leaning on the car for support. Towering over the two men, he flashed his biggest, most charismatic grin, knowing that, just like with the brothers from the Jag, black or white, it was great to be adored and loved by everyone.

"…I just wanted to say goodbye, "the man finished his sentence. His voice was still polite, still respectful. He also flashed his biggest grin as he pulled out a 9mm from under his coat.

With a silencer screwed on you could hardly hear the slight pinging, six rounds fired point blank into the man's chest. Wide-eyed and still smirking slightly, he was dead before he slumped down against the shiny car's front tire.

As his partner stepped over the body to place the gun to the dead man's left temple, more from habit than anything else, the marine snapped an order.

"No! No, it's supposed to look like a robbery, not an execution. Just a plain, simple, run-of-the-mill robbery. The kills next month are the executions, remember? If this was supposed to look like a professional hit I would have done the damn job myself!"

"Take his wallet, the rings…and those gold chains," he ordered, pointing to twenty thousand dollars worth of braided gold around the dead man's neck.

"Man, I don't want to touch the nigger's…"

"Take the chains," the man ordered again. He said it quietly this time, but his tone left no doubt about what he wanted done.

The third man, still sitting rigidly in the back seat of the sedan, adjusted his wire-rimmed glasses and watched his men finish their work. His only reaction was a slight nod when the now ex-NBA superstar collapsed against the front tire of his big new car and his blood began gushing onto the pavement.

It was risky for him to be out here tonight, there was no doubt about that. Just as there was no doubt that this first one was more than a little bit personal for him. But it was his plan that was about to be set in motion, and he wanted to be here at the beginning. He wanted to be able to tell his grandchildren and their grandchildren and all the world's grandchildren that he was there to see the very first drop of blood that had opened the floodgates to a grand new age in American history.

That he was there at the beginning.

Years ago, even as a child, he realized he had been born with a different type mind. An eidetic, or photographic, memory the doctors had so clinically called it in their antiseptic way. Or a picture-book mind as his mother had lovingly referred to it when his playmates were cruelly making fun of the spooky little freak with a mousetrap brain. Years and years of being incredibly burdened with a mind cluttered with every image ever seen and not being able to erase any of it had driven him to the edge of sanity before his true purpose in life was revealed to him.

Now he realized this unbelievable gift was a blessing from God himself, to be used as a tool for his mission here on earth. And a weapon if need be.

And tonight, with that nigger bleeding his useless brains onto the pavement, made for a perfect snapshot for the old family album his mother always so proudly proclaimed lived inside his head.

God had ordained him for this, had prepared him for just this task. Just as he had ordained and prepared Adolf Hitler to purge Europe of the unworthy.

God had made this his calling, his purpose here on earth. God had put pure white men here to rule the earth, not share in its leadership with filth born from the bellies of mongrel bitches. Especially mongrel nigger bitches.

That filth, along with the liberal fools that had driven America to the point of collapse with their unrealistic hogwash about freedom and equal rights and liberty for any damn skin color that simply asked for it, were about to pay for their transgressions in a hard way.

America would rise up from this darkness and bask once again in sunlight.

A pure, white, Arian sunlight.

Despite some rough edges, tonight had been a successful beginning. A successful dress rehearsal for the purifying fire that was to come. All that was left for him was to wrap up some minor problems both here and down south, let his plan swing into full motion, and then sit back and watch the blood flow as a born-again nation was cleansed.

True, the security leaks that had popped up so unexpectedly still bothered him. Lord knows he still brooded over how one single disloyal courier carrying such vitally important information could cause him so much grief. But after praying day and night for guidance he realized that was all water under the bridge now and that his plan must go on. All he could do was plug up the leaks, repair whatever damage had been done, and then learn from this mistake. And who knows, maybe this little mishap was just the Lord's way of letting him know that it wasn't time yet to reveal the harsher aspects of his plan to the others, despite the overwhelming support he had received so far.

The problem in Mexico, this slippery Ricky Simon character, would be silenced quickly. The little magician with a shotgun and a thousand different faces had outfoxed his men so far, true. But he'd committed more than enough resources now to peel away all those disguises to see to the brutal, quick end of one Mr. Ricky Simon. And that would be the end of that leak.

And as for the two private detectives right here in Hollywood he needed for the frame-up and subsequent deal and trade required to get his documents back,, well, he still had use for at least one of them for a while longer. But when his job was done, then he too would meet a brutal, quick end. Along with his mongrel partner.

Looking up to the starlit heavens as if to acknowledge the beginning of greatness, the man nodded at the thought of how incredibly easy all of this could be at times. With that thought he let out a deep sigh and relaxed for the first time tonight. And with that sigh a smile flickered over his gaunt face. A smile that had been a long, long time coming.

A few moments later the sedan pulled out of the parking lot, leaving behind a body and a mystery for the police to find in the morning. A body, a mystery and the opening act of things to come. They turned left at the corner and headed towards the Hollywood freeway, and their home base.

Mission accomplished. A new world was on its way.

CHAPTER 1

The street looked like any other in all the shitholes he'd slipped through over the last twenty years. Boarded-up shops, cars rusting away in the blazing sun, stray dogs and starving kids fighting for their lives over scraps of garbage dumped along the roadside dominated the landscape. The sight of this pathetic gutter and the rancid taste of poverty and shit that hung in the air was nauseating. Even to someone used to it.

Yeah, just another street in just another Mexican shithole. A diseased brown line running from point A to point B.

Except this street had a phone booth at the end of it. And that made all the difference in the world. And even washed away some of that rancid stink of hopelessness. A tiny, faded blue and white booth that was just what he'd been praying for in a land where cell phones never seemed to connect to anything but more useless shit.

He hid behind one of the boarded-up shops, squinting through the heat at the distant phone booth, and looked down at his prisoner on his knees in front of him. Stripped down to his underwear, bloody rag stuffed in his mouth, hands and feet duck-tapped behind him, his eyes told Ricky everything he needed to know. The dumb son of a bitch knew nothing. Not a Goddamn thing at all. But Ricky had to ask anyway, if only to ease his mind a little about what he may be walking into once he stepped out into the street.

"Donde esta Federalies...aqui? Donde esta?"

Then as if to add more emphasis he added in English, Y'know, kid, the cops with the real big fuckin' guns. Where the hell are they?"

"Donde esta, huh?"

The man's only response was the same pathetic shivering and whimpering that had started almost as soon as Ricky caught him following him into the little alley and roughed him up a bit in the hopes of shaking a little information loose. All he got instead was the crying and those sad eyes begging for mercy.

He looked down the street again at the phone booth. It was daylight, and that bothered him. Bothered the hell out of it. Damn, this would have been so much easier at night. He knew he was a sitting duck just hanging here in the alley any longer than he absolutely had to, and he didn't have the luxury of waiting for darkness, so one way of another he was going to have to chance it in broad daylight. But the longer he stared down the street, the more a sense of dread began spreading through him.

The same feeling that been knocking at his door for over a week now.

Hell, it seemed like almost a lifetime ago, but he'd stumbled over the intel that started this shitstorm only a week ago. A snitch he'd used from time to time had come knocking on his door in the middle of the night with some really mind blowing stuff from down south and that one little conversation had kicked all this shit into overdrive. Ricky could tell from the guy's edginess all he wanted was to make a quick score, get some traveling money, and then get the hell out of Dodge. And after hearing what the guy had he understood why. The shit seemed so goddamned unbelievably and completely insane, even to a man like himself who'd been dealing in death most of his life, that he normally would have taken a pass on it. Just zipped his lips and moved on. Problem was, he had more than just a casual interest in one of the names that kept popping up as the snitch laid out the plans to him. A name that was on a list of people to be wasted before this baby took off full speed and exploded on the world. So he pushed the snitch hard to get him more. He pushed real damn hard.

That was his first mistake. He should have been content with what he already had. But he pushed for more. Unfortunately, the snitch paid the price. Two days after their first meeting the man vanished as if he'd fallen off the face of the earth. It didn't take a goddamn genius to figure out what happened to him.

Then he made his second mistake. And this one really hurt. Instead of getting the hell out of Dodge himself, he put the word out and tried to buy that one name off the list. That turned out to be an unbelievably stupid move. But how the fuck was he to know all his money didn't mean squat to these guys? And if they didn't already know who the dead snitch was selling his little goodies to, they sure as hell did now. He couldn't have led them to him any better if he'd painted a goddamn yellow brick road leading right to his front door and laid out milk and cookies for them along the way.

Now he was on the run like a rabid dog. So far he'd killed four of the well-dressed punks in three-piece suits. Blasted them all with a shotgun at point blank range. Funny thing was, it didn't seem to bother the rest of the wolfpack one fuckin' bit. And it sure didn't stop them from goose-stepping around like they owned every place they hit, either. Despite some close scrapes his luck had held, at least until now, that is. He was still alive to sing like a goddamn songbird about what he'd stumbled across.

Not that he particularly wanted to.

The whispers about some very public executions of some dumb shit niggers who had somehow managed to forge some kind of bullshit alliance with al Qaeda terrorists by pouring hundreds of millions of dollars into their cause – Blaq-Qaeda - was what the black boys were calling this new alliance, and then some terrorist crap by these new boys in retaliation for those killings that was supposed to make the Twin Towers hit look like a Sunday wienie roast, meant nothing to him. Absolutely nothing at all. If the goddamn US of A wanted to tear itself to pieces playing chicken shit little racial games, then, hell, let it. Black against white, white against black. Spicks, niggers, rednecks, chinks, kykes, Japs, wops, wetbacks. None of that shit meant diddley squat to him.

But that one little name that was somehow tied into all these wild plans by some sort of "deal and trade" bullshit certainly did.

The name Charles Alexander Custer would always mean something to him. Hell, he owed it to the man, for all the times he'd saved his ass when he was nothing more than a dumb-ass rookie with a badge and a gun who thought he could change the world by playing by the rules, that if he couldn't buy his name off that list, then at least he could stick his neck out just a little bit further and try to warn him about the tidal wave of shit rushing his way.

So far, he'd survived two massive mistakes on his part and was still standing. But they definitely had managed to rattle the shit out of him. So what he needed now was just a little more time to contact Charlie and then digging a real deep hole and burying himself in it for a long, long time seemed like a real good idea to him.

And he had absolutely no problem letting these rumors about all this Blaq-Qaeda bullshit and firebombed colleges and napalmed kids and Marshall Law and segregated regions and niggers going back to the back of the bus go quietly underground with him.

But getting the word to his old partner hadn't proved to be as simple as it first sounded. Which was exactly why his own ass was still way too damn much above ground at the moment. He'd tried day and night since his name first came up, but the man, no longer one of L.A. finest but now an ass-kicking private dick with a sky high profile, was nowhere to be found. Almost as if he too had fallen off the face of the earth. Just like the snitch he'd pumped too hard..

Ricky hated to even think about it. But it was beginning to look more and more like it was a case of too little too goddamn late. And that maybe the only ass now left to save was his own raggedy one.

Crouching now behind the boarded-up shop with a faded Coca Cola logo out front like one of the scrawny mutts roaming the street in front of him, Ricky bowed his head at the thought of his friend's death. He knew it had to be ugly. And violent.

But then he reminded himself of the man and his own violent ways that had been his calling card down through the years.

Charles A. Custer was without question the toughest son of a bitch he'd ever known. A man who, like the rookie cop he'd trained and then rode with for twelve years in a black and white only to see him end up on the FBI's most wanted list, always covered his fuckin' ass. Always. So maybe, just maybe, he'd gotten wind of what was coming down, or maybe he'd gotten out of a few tight spots with these assholes himself, and then dug himself a nice little rabbit hole and simply faded off everyone's radar. Much like Ricky himself was planning to do.

It was a long shot, but sometimes long shots are all you get in this crappy world.

And as if he didn't have enough on his mind already, another troubling aspect of Charlie's disappearance - troubling because he just might need this guy's help himself if all else turned to shit - was that somewhere along the line Custer had taken on an aging drunken beach bum as his prized protégé. A fuckin' surfer-boy, for Christ sake! Why the hell L.A.'s most famous private dick would pick a drunken fuck up to cover his ass was anyone's guess, but for the moment Ricky could only chalk it up to fate. Fate and a real bad sense of timing on the surfer's part, because for whatever reason, his name was on that list, too.

So on the slim chance Charlie was still alive, his plan now was to call the kid, pray that he was sober, and then somehow convince him to hit the bricks in an effort to scare up Charlie and play messenger for him.

Because after tonight, with or without Charlie Custer, one Ricky Simon was making a bee line straight for the Brazilian bush, where phones and hopefully assholes in three-piece suits were about as rare as blond, blue-eyed ladies. That being his future, then this just might be his last chance to save the only real friend he had left in this world. He could only pray this Aaron Ireland stiff would be sober enough to remember what he was told. And then do the fuckin' job like the pro the cocky little son of a bitch had everyone on the planet believing he was.

The man whimpering in front of him brought Ricky back to his more immediate problem. Hell, the guy was probably the only honest cop in Mexico. A guy with a fat, bitchy wife and a half dozen mongrel kids who thought he was protecting his shithole town when he'd followed him into this alley.

Unfortunately, that was a mistake he'd never survive.

Quietly pulling out a 12 inch blade from his waistband, he knelt in front of the crying man, and for a brief second thought he saw forgiveness in his eyes. It was over in a split second and as Ricky wiped the bloody blade on his pants he looked over at the man's uniform folded neatly on the ground nearby.

Unbuttoning his shirt, Ricky Simon looked once more at the phone booth at the far end of the dirty little town's main drag. Ha! Main drag, that term always killed him when they used it down here. Hell, him and Charlie had walked down bigger alleys in Hollywood as cops than this pathetic little line of shit. And they'd walked them with ass-kicking pride. Because, at one time, they had been the good guys.

"Yeah, the good guys…" Ricky whispered, then smiled sadly.

Dressed in the khaki uniform of the local policia, with a huge drooping mustache covering up the telltale scar on his left cheek, Ricky Simon stepped out boldly into the street.

In broad daylight.

CHAPTER 2

The phone rang in the dark apartment. And kept on ringing until a hand from the body that was laying curled up on the floor slapped it across the apartment. The apartment's other occupant, a huge sheepdog, bounded after the flying phone, dodging what looked like a well planned obstacle course of empty tequila bottles and crushed beer cans, to rush to where it had landed and brought it back to where the silent body was already curled up in a ball again. The animal dropped the phone near the body and pawed at it several times and then waited, hoping for praise for a job well done. And maybe even another chance at chasing it. Seeing no sign of life, she eventually gave up and settled down next to the body.

The body began coughing and finally came to life several minutes later. The man eventually sat upright and leaned back against the wall. Taking a deep breath, he casually leaned over and threw up into a waiting bucket. Something he had been doing way too much lately.

"Too much tequila, Calvin", he slurred at the sheepdog. "Way too much fuckin' tequila, man."

The dog moaned in response, as if in total agreement.

His head was killing him, and his face, well his face felt like it always did these days. It hurt like a motherfucker.

Instinctively his hand reached up to the left side of his face where a white gauze bandage covered most of the area from his left eye to his jaw. He knew the white gauze was probably now streaked with sick looking red stains because he knew the damned wound was always bleeding. Still bleeding after a month. Christ, that had to be some kind of goddamn record somewhere. His hand touching the wet bandage only confirmed it for him. Even that slight touch of the wet gauze made him sick, and he leaned over and puked into the bucket again.

Wiping his mouth with his shirt sleeve, he smiled grimly to himself. And then reached over and gently patted the huge white head of his friend.

Yeah, that was the price he'd paid for stopping the killing spree that had swept through Hollywood and ended once and for all the now almost legendary "Jack the Ripper" murders. Now good ol' Hollywood and its endless parade of teenage hookers could go about their business in relative safety. Free from the fear of mutilation by razor blades, sliced off fingers and a final resting place inside a dumpster somewhere along Sunset Bl dressed up in a satin robe. And he got an eternally painful and permanent reminder of a completely chance meeting in a dark alley with an insane serial killer and his really big knife.

But he had stopped the killing. And most nights, alone in his apartment with an endless supply of tequila and old Marvin Gay records, it didn't seem to be such a bad trade-off for a fucked up face.

But he had to admit he was more than just a little bit edgy about what life had in store for him once the bandages were finally stripped away to reveal a face that looked just a little bit too much like Frankenstein's older brother.

Yeah, just add on a few rusty bolts jutting out from his temples and he'd fit in real good in the old doc's lab. Just a few fuckin' bolts and he'd be set for life.

The phones' ringing again shook him from his morbid thoughts. Even half drunk, he knew exactly who was calling and exactly what the hell they wanted.

After a month he would have thought his fight in that alley and the girl he'd rescued in the process would be old news. But, hell no, because the goddanm reporters just wouldn't let this thing die a natural death. Now his fifteen minutes of fame had turned into a nightmare that showed absolutely no signs of dying. Or even slowing down for that matter.

And he had to admit he was at least partially to blame for that.

In the beginning, right after the alley when he was still on an adrenalin rush and acting cocky and just plain stupid, he'd screwed around with the reporters, egging them on as he gave what he thought were some absolutely fabulous interviews. Christ, did he ever play the swashbuckling super hero to the hilt! Hard drinkin', hard drivin', hard boiled super dick hero that he was! And he had absolutely no problem soaking in all the glory as he was proclaimed by every damn newspaper and magazine in the country as the new face of justice in America.

Hell, he thought he had those dumb-shit reporters and all of America by the balls back then. Like he could turn them on and off like some goddamn light switch.

The reality was that he was just too goddamn dumb to realize all he was doing was pouring gas all over himself for the eventual bonfire that was sure to come. Now he was absolutely powerless to stop them from doing what they did best. And that, of course, was creating some very entertaining and thrilling stories based on "eyewitness" accounts about fearless super dick Aaron Ireland and the life he'd devoted to fighting crime on the mean streets of L.A. And all the terrible wrongs he'd righted with just the wink of an eye on those very streets.

Yeah, Aaron Ireland, bad-ass knight in shining armor with a resume full of ass-kickings and beat-downs.

It was all bullshit.

Just like the stuff he'd fed them in the beginning.

Picking up the phone he cut loose with a string of obscenities to punish any fuckin' reporter. Or anyone with a picture perfect face, for that matter.

A woman's soft voice quickly ended the assault.

"Oh my God…Christina… is that really you?" he slurred. He couldn't believe it, after a month and all the crazy things that had happened since he'd last heard her voice, she'd finally called.

"I've called you a million times …I can't believe you finally called back. My God, I'm just so glad…y'know, you wouldn't believe everything that's happened…"

"Aaron, look, I only called to ask you to quit calling me, ok?" Her voice was flat and businesslike. "It's gotten pretty much out of hand, don't you think?"

"I know, I know…I'm sorry for that, but I just wanted…"

"It's over between us, Aaron," she cut him off, her voice losing a little of that hard edge and faltering a little. Half-drunk, Aaron could sense the hesitation in it. And the possible chance it held for him.

"Come on, honey. It can't be over just like that. After all, y'know, your boyfriend's a big hero now, …you wouldn't want to just walk away just when things are getting' interesting, would you?" he boomed with drunken confidence.

"Yeah…that's the problem, Aaron. You're this really big celebrity now and…"

"No, no, honey…I'm really not!" he shot back, quickly realizing the mistake he'd made in trying to impress her with his press clippings.

"It's just those damn reporters and those silly little stories they keep cooking up. Hell, you know me. You know most of that stuff is just garbage anyway…"

"You've changed, Aaron," she cut him off again, her voice instantly back to the business tone at the mention of his celebrity status. "And not for the better!"

"Gosh, every time I turn on the TV or pick up a magazine or read a newspaper or…or anything… there you are…telling the whole world what a big hero you are and how exciting it was beating up that guy in that alley and how you saved all of Hollywood and practically the entire planet all by yourself," she paused for a second, "and how you, all by yourself, outsmarted the police, the FBI and everyone else and caught the 'Ripper' killer!"

"Well, I did catch him, y'know. And the rest of that stuff, all that bravado and all the braggin', well, Christ, that's just for my fans, y'know…"

"Your fans," she blurted out. "My God, Aaron, what's happened to you? Inside that conceited little brain of yours you do know that you didn't really catch Jack The Ripper, don't you? Not the real one anyway. All you did was catch a mixed-up little psycho!"

"Well, yeah…of course I know that!"

"Don't you see, Aaron. My God, you've changed so much. I can't even talk to you anymore. The guy I fell in love with was just a nice easy going guy who took every day as it came and could care less about TV cameras and magazine covers…A guy I used to be able to talk to about anything for hours on end …" she seemed to be on the verge of crying as she talked about how he used to be.

"Hey, all I did was take a job with Charlie to impress your dad…" Aaron quietly broke in, almost seeing her tears. "And everything else that happened, well, just sort of happened."

"The great Charles Custer…God, Aaron, do you have any idea how much I hate that name?" she spat. "If it wasn't for your little buddy none of this would have happened…"

"Oh, and by the way…where's your old Mustang? You know, the one you said you'd keep forever...the one that Steve whatshisname drove in that 'Bullett' movie you're always watching."

"All I ever see you in now is that stupid red Mercedes convertible. With that redheaded whore climbing all over you!"

A long, strained silence followed as Aaron knew he was busted. He didn't have the faintest hint that she was keeping track of him, let alone her knowing about the redhead and the ball-bustin' relationship he had going on with her.

"The Mercedes was a gift from, ah, one of my fans. No strings attached, y'know, just a little present for me giving him kind of a 'grand tour' of the alley where it all happened," he said slowly, knowing all too well how pathetic it probably sounded to her. "He just wanted to see where all the action happened, that's all."

"And…" she pushed the issue.

"And the redhead is…a…y'know…I don't really know…she's, ah, kinda like a client, I guess." He paused again. "She wants me to do something for her, and I'm not sure that I can…or want too…

"Yeah, Aaron, I bet she wants you to do something for her!" the sarcasm dripped from her voice. "I just bet she does!

"You know, Aaron, you're really a jerk!"

"Look, Christina…honey, it's not like that at all…it's really not. It's all part of this 'Ripper' thing."

"Yeah, Aaron, I just bet it is! So she's all just part of something that's already over and done with, right?" she laughed. "My God, Aaron, just how stupid do you think I am?"

After a long pause, he finally mumbled. "No…no, it really is part of the murders…but sort of like a separate deal…"

"You know, Aaron, even when my father thought you were nothing more than a drunken old bum who surfed all day and partied all night, at least he said you were a nice bum who had manners… and was honest.." The sarcasm and anger were gone for good now, replaced again by tears. And a plea.

"Please…please don't call me again. It's over…please just let it be over."

The aching in her voice told him it was really over. He waited a second before asking one last thing.

"Just tell me one thing," he asked softly. "Tell me it isn't because of what happened to my face…"

"Oh God, Aaron…believe me, this has nothing to do with that. You've just changed so much…" She was crying hard now, not even trying to control it.

"What happened to your face has nothing to do with this, believe me…nothing at all."

With that the line went dead and he was alone again in the dark.

After a few moments of sitting in the dark, he realized that it really was over for her. For the first time since he'd met her on the beach that day two years ago when she'd mistakenly thought he was one of her girlfriend's dad, he had lied to her. And she knew it. She was just too damn nice and too damn classy to shove it down his throat like he so richly deserved. Yeah, she knew he was fucking the redhead. And probably knew it from day one. And she probably knew, or at least had a real good educated guess, that all the little teen whores Charlie had sent him out to interview for him in hopes of turning up some clue that he'd initially missed, he'd been fucking them too just as much as he'd been questioning them.

He'd lost her because he was just as much of a whore as the ones who'd been butchered by 'The Ripper'. Because he couldn't keep his damn dick in his pants even when he'd finally met the woman of his dreams.

Yeah, a very not so private dick was what he really was.

Thinking of what he'd lost, his hand automatically went up to his face and felt the moist gauze. Yeah, Christ, he wouldn't have to worry about meeting the woman of his dreams again.

Not with a face like this, that was for damn sure.

Leaning over, he puked into the bucket again. And then reached for the bottle of tequila that never left his side these days.

CHAPTER 3

The sign was perfect. And the placement of it was a stroke of genius.

Pure genius. The battle cry "Nigger Go Home" never looked so good hanging around a dead man's neck, he was sure of that. In bright red ink and scrawled in huge child-like letters, no plantation owner could have done it up better. Or been more proud. And hiding the man's face with an old burlap bag over his head and a noose around his neck only added to the genius of it.

Yeah, mixing a lynching scene with high tech 9mm bullet holes really gave it the retro look he was after.

Finally the real action had begun. In just four short weeks they had managed to kill seven of these fuckin' animals. Nine, no ten, really, if you counted the first two or three they were forced to make look like robberies. Just your everyday violence in America.

But now the real deal was flowing!

"Just like your blood, asshole!" the man spat, before ramming the gun into the burlap where the man's forehead was hidden and jerking off another round. "Flowin' just like your nigger blood!"

"Hey, Bobby, you think I should maybe cut some eyeholes in the sack, you know, to make it look like he saw the whole thing? Or at least saw his boys go down first?" he pointed to the man's two bodyguards laying face down near their car, handcuffed, with a bullet in each head. "I think maybe that would look kinda cool, ya know…"

Turning to stroll back to the car where his partner waited, he couldn't help but feel a sense of satisfaction, and pride, wash over his body.

Yeah man, the real deal was definitely flowin'!

CHAPTER 4

"I love you too, sweetheart. Have a safe flight, and say hello to your mother for me." The voice was soft and loving as he hung up the phone just as tenderly. A smile came over the man's face, lacing his fingers behind his head as he leaned back in his leather chair to picture her in his mind. God, he loved his little angel! There wasn't anything in the world he wouldn't do for her. Nothing, absolutely nothing. And there wasn't anyone he wouldn't kill to protect her from this brutal world they lived in.

In fact, he already was doing just that. He nodded to himself, the smile fading as he thought again about the task, the awesome responsibility, he had been blessed with.

"Sir, the White House on line one…"

The Director of the CIA stopped his nodding to look up at the secretary pecking in cautiously through his doorway.

"Tell them I will return their call later today." Carefully adjusting his wire rim glasses, he waved her off for what seemed like the thousandth time this morning.

"Ah, sir, this is their third call…this time it's the President himself…"

"I will return his call later today," he repeated. He spoke firmer now, his voice still not rising above his usual whisper-like level but sarcasm edging into the usually unemotional tone. "Later today…if that's okay with you, of course…"

As the secretary backed meekly out of the doorway, J. Jonathan Downey's thoughts returned to his daughter.

He truly was doing his part to make this world a better place for her. He was certain of that. And if it hadn't been for what was really her only mistake in her twenty precious years on the planet, he might never have realized his true calling that the Lord himself had placed squarely in front of him since his appointment as Director.

His little angel had started dating him during her junior year. A big, lazy black buck whose entire career aspirations centered on stardom in the NBA and then maybe some sort of rap career garbage after that. Good

God, the dumb son-of-a-bitch couldn't even talk in complete sentences, only that hip-hop rhyme crap! And with his hair in ridiculous looking braids, or "corn rows" as she had proudly called them, he looked even dumber than he was, if that was even humanly possible. And yet his little girl was supposedly in love with this jungle bunny.

The thought of them together, him caressing her with his thick, puffy lips and raw black paws and her foundling him back, made him sick to his stomach. More than once his migraines had become so severe that he had to be hospitalized. And his ulcers, good God, he didn't even want to think about the way they had acted up, practically bleeding through the entire ordeal of their courtship. If that's what you wanted to call their sick attraction to each other.

And not to be lost or overlooked by his own pain, the complete, total humiliation spewed on him from the high brow Washington circles he swam in was just as crippling as any physical pain he'd been forced to endure.

Three months later she was pregnant with the nigger's baby and the black bastard was nowhere in sight. Gee, what a surprise that was! A nigger doing what a nigger does best! Supposedly he'd dropped out of school to prepare himself for the NBA draft and the life of riches that lay ahead, or at least that's what he told her. But after a few months of not returning her frantic calls, calls, his little angel finally got the hint that he'd used her the same way niggers use all white women.

But the Lord giveth and the Lord taketh away.

The black bastard with the braided hair had his useless life ended right in front of his shiny new car in a Hollywood parking lot not more than four weeks ago. Now the nigger was burning in Hell for his sins, J. Jonathan Downey was sure of that. And, praise the Lord, he had been there to witness it.

The Lord's will shall be done. And J. Jonathan Downey was proud to be the one enforcing that will.

"Ah, sir…I really hate to keep bothering you…but the President keeps calling and…"

"It's ok. I'll take his call now," the Director whispered.

Ever since the killings had begun in earnest, going from random hold-ups to outright assassinations, the White House and its mongrel leader had been knocking down his door trying to get any information he might have about possible terrorist ties to the killings. That thought made him smile. Of course he knew nothing about that, sir. Nothing at all, sir. Yes sir, I agree, this is absolutely horrible, sir.

But give it a few more weeks and the next questions would be about Black America's probable, not possible, mind you, but probable involvement with al-Qaeda terrorists and probable new targets on American soil.

Yes, the Lord giveth. And the Lord certainly does taketh.

And so does J. Jonathan Downey.

CHAPTER 5

The phone rang again in the dark apartment. Almost like déjà vu. But time had passed and he knew it wasn't her calling. He'd tried to stay sober in the hopes she'd call again, but as the days passed and hope faded he went back to his routine that consisted mainly of booze and more booze and then staring at his butchered face in the mirror. And hanging out with the redhead, who he guessed was no great secret to anyone anymore. Picking up the phone he thought about not answering it, as he had started to do more and more of, or maybe just slapping it off the wall again. After ten rings he finally flipped it open just to stop the racket.

But one word, the one word the man on the other end of the line managed to sneak in as Aaron began his assault on who he was certain was just another jack-ass reporter, instantly brought Aaron's assault to a halt.

Custer.

Charles A. Custer. The famous name of the nearly legendary man who had mysteriously vanished halfway through the case, dropping completely out of sight weeks before Aaron and the killer had their rendezvous in that alley.

"What do you know about Charlie?" Aaron asked slowly.

"I know he's not in that shithole of a bar you two guys call home. Hasn't stepped foot in there in weeks. Hasn't been anywhere else around L.A., either," the mysterious voice said quietly, then paused.

"And I know you've been lookin' for him in your half-assed pissy litttle way and haven't come up with dog shit. But ya know what I think, kid? I think maybe you been too damn busy soakin' up the glory and the booze and so interested in gettin' your dick sucked by that hot little redheaded bitch to really do a decent job of tryin' to find anyone."

"That's what I think, kid."

Not getting an immediate answer, the man pressed on in a hard, raspy voice that sounded mean, and impatient. Maybe a little nervous, too. It also sounded very much in control.

"And I know I need to talk to Charlie Custer now. Right now. Like fuckin' pronto, kid. And I know that if you don't do exactly what I say, do exactly what I want, you're gonna have a few more real nasty lookin' scars tearin' up that other side of your goddamn face to match those big, ugly sons-of-bitches you're cryin' about now! You got that? Am I makin' myself clear, kid?

"Am I makin' myself clear, kid?" He repeated the words slowly.

A moment of silence passed as Aaron sucked on the man's words. And got more pissed off as they rattled around his tequila-drenched brain.

The stranger on the other end continued on matter-of-factly after the pause, as if his last remarks had never been spoken. As if he made threats like this casually, a thousand times a day, and then went on with business as usual. Business as usual, as long as he got what he wanted.

"Sometime in the next few days you're gonna get a fuckin'envelope that has instructions and a plane ticket. I repeat, instructions and a plane ticket. For Charlie Custer. No one else, kid, y'understand? Jus' Custer. Now you're gonna go out and find Charlie for me and give him that goddamn envelope."

He paused for a second and blew out a deep breath that Aaron could almost feel through the phone. "Now I gone through a lotta shit these last few weeks jus' tryin' to get you to answer your goddamn phone, so you are gonna find him for me!

"Do you understand me, kid?" he repeated deliberately, as if Aaron were partially deaf, or maybe just beginning his first day of kindergarten. "I don't care what it takes, or what you gotta do to dig him up, but you stay outta the goddamn limelight and keep your dick in your pants until you've made goddamn good and sure that Charlie Custer's on that fuckin' plane and...."

"Look, asshole…I didn't ask for any of this shit ..." Aaron burst out. All he wanted his old life back, dragging down Sunset Bl. in his old Steve McQueen fastback with Christina by his side, and he was sick and tired of explaining that to every reporter in the goddamned world. He didn't need the Mercedes convertible and the empty headed nymph that had replaced them. He was sick of it all. And he was goddamn sick of explaining himself to assholes who only wanted a story out of him.

"Tell you what, buddy. If you're serious about wanting to take a few whacks at fuckin' my face up a little more, then please, just trot you dumb ass on over here and take your best shot, okay! I'm here, I'm awake, thanks to your dumb ass, and I got nothin' but time on my hands.

"But if that isn't in your plans tonight, then why don't you just knock off the goddamn threats and that tough guy attitude of yours, and tell me what you really want, okay? Stop with all the big mystery bullshit or hang up the damn phone and let me get back to my beauty sleep, okay?"

"Am I makin' myself clear, kid?" Aaron slowly drawled what seemed to be the guy's favorite expression. He was drunk and pissed off and to him the painfully slow imitation sounded absolutely perfect.

Another long moment of silence came and went. Just as Aaron was about to hang up, the man sighed deeply and spoke again. This time his voice had an almost sad tone to it that startled Aaron.

"It's about your death, kid. Yours and Charlie's."

"What?"

"Look, kid, my time's runnin' out and I don't want to get into this over the phone, okay? You just do me a tiny little favor and go out like a good little Boy Scout and dig up Charlie for me, and you tell him that Ricky Simon needs to talk to him..."

Aaron's jaw dropped at the mention of that name.

"Ricky Simon my motherfuckin' ass!" he yelled. Then he threw the phone against the apartment's far wall. A second later it broke apart as it bounced off the wall.

By the anger in his voice, and the way the phone exploded after it hit the wall, Calvin the sheepdog knew better than to play fetch this time. He played it safe and stayed curled up in the corner instead.

Reporters! Jesus fuckin' Christ! There just seemed to be no end to what they would do to keep a story alive! As soon as you think they couldn't possibly sink any lower, they dig up a whole new pile of bullshit to ram down your throat!

And using Ricky Simon's name was one pile of bullshit Aaron Ireland never saw coming.

Hell yeah, he knew the name. So did every damn cop in the country. From his early days as a wet-behind-the-ears rookie to the end when he ripped off countless millions in dope from the police property room and then sold the shit to the very same scum he'd put behind bars, and all the good years and good deeds in-between, Aaron knew all about Ricky Simon.

From a thousand drunken nights in a thousand different bars with Charlie, hell yeah, he knew all about Ricky Simon.

Sometimes with complete disgust in his voice, and then sometimes with an almost awestruck admiration, Charlie Custer could never stop talking about his ex-partner. And best friend.

Yeah, Aaron knew all about Ricky Simon.

He also knew that Ricky Simon had been killed several years ago in a fiery Mexican car crash. A very well publicized fact that some goddamn ignorant little reporter had apparently neglected to punch up on his nifty little computer.

CHAPTER 6

The casket was ornate and expensive. The polished wood and brass gleamed in the snow despite the gentle flakes pelting it. Sticking out like it did in the peaceful, park-like cemetery, it was obvious that it was much too ornate and much too expensive for the tiny gathering of friends and relatives who attended the graveside service.

After all, she was just a whore. A common tramp who died in a very violent way in a very violent city that no one in this peaceful setting cared to know anything about. It didn't matter who her father was or how many drug cartels or politicians he had in his pocket. A whore was a whore. The fact was she'd probably gotten exactly what she deserved, razor blade and all.

The last two remaining men from the brief service stood ten feet apart, but the snow falling between them could easily have covered a thousand miles instead of just a few feet.

The shorter, squat, pig-like man with the sagging jowls and overflowing belly was the whore's father. He leaned casually against a tree, obviously not interested in the least in the service that had just ended. At times he would pick at his stubby fingernails with a pocketknife as if the entire ceremony had been one long, poorly made movie he'd been forced to sit through. His daughter's death meant little to him and the quick funeral service, almost like a Las Vegas wedding with its rapid-paced proficiency, meant even less.

The second man, older, and graying in the dignified way of a career military officer, or a corporate CEO, knelt rigidly beside the casket, crossing himself as he wept. Even in heartbreaking grief, the man instinctively acted like a good Catholic, offering prayers of salvation over his granddaughter's grave.

Along with prayers of forgiveness for allowing something like this to happen.

But the moment he finished mumbling Father, Son, and Holy Ghost, Charlie Custer wondered if any of it was true. Was there a God? Or a Heaven? Or was this hell on earth meant to be just what it appeared to be: one long endless parade of one funeral after another, with just tiny shreds of pathetic happiness squeezed in between.

Only now even those shreds were gone. The girl in the coffin was simply the last in that long, ugly parade.

It was over forty years that his son had come home from Vietnam in a body bag. The boy had been only nineteen when the yellow telegram arrived announcing that their only son had stepped on a booby-trap and died in a medi-vac chopper on the way to a hospital in DaNang

A second telegram came a few days later, very officially informing them that the body would not be fit for viewing. It contained words about explosions and amputations and other things that didn't make any sense to him or his wife.

At the time, even as a street cop in the middle of his own war, Charlie Custer couldn't picture in his mind what had happened to his son. So he kept digging and eventually forced himself to find out about explosions and booby-traps and traumatic amputations and the unbelievable horrors that a pound of hot lead can do to a teenage body.

Six months later his wife took her own life. His beautiful Claire, found laying peacefully on the living room sofa with her brains dripping on the carpet and ugly black powder burns scorching her forehead.

In a sick twist of irony, she had used his own service revolver to blow her beautiful brains out. Just one quick .38 slug to the right temple and all her pain was over. It seemed funny, in a sick way, because he'd had those very same thoughts over and over again himself ever since that telegram came. But for some reason, only fragile Claire had the guts to pull the trigger.

He retired from the Department the day after the funeral and devoted himself entirely to his new career of sucking down Jack Daniels as hard and as fast as he could.

Then, in a stroke of fate that amazed him even today, just when it seemed like his life was completely flushed down the shitter, another ex-cop rescued him. An ex-SWAT captain with a booming private detective business who'd hunted him down for a few questions about a run-of-the-mill kidnapping case he'd worked on years ago.

And just like that he was back in it.

He tackled the detective business like a snarling bulldog, determined to make the world right again. He had an idea he was still drinking too much, but hell, even snarling bulldogs get lonely at night.

And as long as the booze and the loneliness didn't dominate his life like before, he could live with it.

What mattered was he was back doing the one thing he was good at. Back trying to save the world, one case at a time.

And even when the last remaining tie to all he once had, his daughter, died during child-birth after a gut-wrenching marriage to a squatty little pig who used her as his own private punching bag whenever his days of wheeling and dealing in drugs and prostitution didn't go quite right, he'd slipped back into the Jack full time for only a little while.

And then there was the darling baby girl left behind. The beautiful, wide-eyed child who from the very first moment he saw her reminded him of his wife. That smile and those shining eyes couldn't possibly belong to anyone but his Claire.

And now, all these years later, that little girl was dead too. Beaten, raped and passed around like a piece of candy by her loving father to impress his cartel buddies, just like he'd done to her mother so many years before, she'd finally summoned up the courage to hit the road. Only that road ended up with her butchered like a sacrificial lamb along Sunset Blvd. like the five teenage whores who came before her. And when the cutting was mercifully over, his granddaughter with the beautiful smile and shining eyes was tossed like so much junk into a garbage bin to rot with a cross stuffed up her privates.

And he could have prevented the whole goddamn thing if he'd found her in time.

He was supposed to be tough and fair, and goddamn, he was. But he didn't have a crystal ball! How the hell was he supposed to know she was in L.A.? Of all the places she could have picked, with all the money she had managed to squirrel away over the years from her trust fund, how the hell could he'd guessed she'd run to L.A.?

But she was there alright, up to her ass in the grim world of teenage porn. Complete with her own mink-coated pimp and hornier-than-hell clients who undoubtedly pumped her fresh young body like there was no goddamn tomorrow. The thought of his innocent, pure honor student turning tricks was so unthinkable to him, so utterly incomprehensible that, even now, none of it made any damn sense to him.

And in another sick twist of fate, not quite as shattering as his wife using his own .38 to kill herself, but almost as sweet, Sara's life came to an end in a garbage dumpster smack dab in the rear of his office building. Not more than fifty feet from his impressively lettered door and its promise of help to anyone who needed it.

No matter how right the excuses sounded about not having crystal balls and all that other logical bullshit, one fact always pounded through: he could have prevented it if he'd found her in time.

Up until now, he'd managed to survive his son's death, and his wife's, and his daughter's, by telling himself over and over again that there really wasn't a damn thing he could have done to stop any of them. He couldn't have gone to Vietnam to protect Bobby for thirteen months. He knew that. He believed that. Just as he knew and believed that nothing or no one could have patched-up Claire's broken mind after that yellow telegram had torn it apart. And God knows he wasn't a delivery room surgeon on that rainy night in December when Sara was born two months early.

But he was a damn good detective. A pro who practically specialized in finding lost little girls. But when the time came, the great Charles A. Custer couldn't even find the one lost little girl who mattered most to him.

Even when she was hiding in his own backyard.

Yeah, out of all of them, this was the one he could have prevented.

And with this eating away at his soul like battery acid, he knew he couldn't do this kind of work anymore.

And as if just to prove that it was high time for him to move on to something else because his mind just wasn't what it once was, somewhere deep in his booze-soaked brain he'd thought he knew who'd killed little Sara and the parade of other teenage whores.

It was years ago, or no, maybe just a few funerals back, but he'd seen those hacked-up tits and those flowing black robes before. The cross was definitely a new touch, but those missing ring fingers really clinched it for him.

He knew the bastard back then - and it was the same man, then and now.

But like so many other times when he'd been hitting the booze hard, he was completely wrong. It still ate away at him to think he could have been so wrong about the whole damn thing. Hell, all those hand carved bloody signs were like glaring signposts pointing him in only one direction. Or at least that's what he'd thought at the time.

But to his everlasting surprise, his pal Aaron had turned the world completely upside down by cornering the right guy in one of those little out of the way alleys that honeycombed through Hollywood and then banged the punk into submission.

And this little psycho wasn't anything close to who Charlie had pegged as the killer.

"Well, whadda say, Chas? You ready to get the hell outta here?" the fat man leaning against the tree smirked. He carefully folded up the pocket knife and put it away to show that it was indeed time to move on to bigger and better things.

Charles Custer slowly crossed himself again. This time he mumbled those words, reverently now, and prayed to have the strength not to kill the pig talking to him. At least not yet. He'd killed other men in his lifetime, but always in the line of duty and usually during a crime. With this asshole here, he didn't need that excuse. All he needed was to see him smile, just one more time.

CHAPTER 7

He carefully adjusted his glasses and allowed himself a slight sigh of relief. And the smallest of smiles. It was finished. From the very first kill to the badly scrawled "nigger go home" to the final professionally written "BLAQ-QAEDA", Phase One was complete. From the first few hits masqueraded as simple random killings to the ones targeting nigger basketball stars to the final one showing America just who they needed to protect themselves against, Phase One was finally over.

He smiled again, much larger now, as he looked at the last one. Yeah, he was a star and wealthy and a headliner in that nigger league, but that wasn't what got him selected for this final honor. No, it was his mouth, as much as anything, that had made him the perfect choice to announce this terrifying new alliance between black America and al-Qaeda. He had railed on and on about America's illegal war in Iraq, about how we were treating our soldiers, as well as the Iraqui people, like common slaves from the good old days. About how terrorists, especially the brave souls who hit the Twin Towers, were really the true heroes of this new day and age and he even predicted dire consequences for the US if we didn't stop trying to hunt down these simple men of passion and pride.

He couldn't have played into their hands any better even if they'd written the script for him.

He really was the perfect choice.

But so was the white man slumped next to him, his agent. Or super-agent, as he had called himself just tonight on a local news show. He had just finished negotiating the richest sports contract in history for his client, with well over two hundred million in guaranteed bonus money now sitting in his client's bank account. Money which would be magically transferred to an off shore bank account with terrorist's ties, just to further prove his connection to his al-Qaeda buddies. The sign hanging from his neck, also professionally printed, warned whites what lay ahead if they too foolishly took up partnerships with Blaq-Qaeda members.

:Ah, sir…we really need to leave the area. You know how risky it is to be here, especially with this being such a busy street and all."

The slightly built man adjusted his wire rim glasses again and nodded in agreement. He looked for one more moment at the two men with signs around their necks and bullet holes in their foreheads. Two men, one black and one white, sitting at a bus stop at the corner of Sunset and Western in Hollywood. From the first kill in a deserted parking lot to this busy bus stop, America now had a new name to focus on and fret over.

Over and over again.

CHAPTER 8

The drive in the limo from the cemetery to the mansion was silent and short. And now sitting on the plush leather sofa in the study of the monstrous house and surrounded by priceless paintings and ungodly expensive Oriental rugs and probably the finest liquor in the world, Charlie Custer fought the urge to vomit. Sitting with his head bowed between his legs, his right hand rested quietly on the gun underneath his tweed jacket.

Cecil Watts had lied through his perfect white teeth to get him here after the funeral. There was no doubt about that. He'd concocted some foolish gibberish about how he'd just happened to stumble across a box full of little Sara's personal things and how he knew good old Grandpa Charlie would love to have for all those lonely days that lay ahead.

It was bullshit, every last lying word of it. Charlie knew it. And Watts knew he knew it. And lying like a little schoolgirl about it just pissed Charlie off more. Sure, he might have thrown together some of Sara's things for Charlie to take back with him, but that was just a pathetic attempt at breaking the ice before they got down to the real business at hand.

Ever since Sara disappeared last year, and the sickening thought finally cracked through Charlie's thick skull that Watts and his pals had been abusing her the very same way they'd abused her mother, he'd come gunning for Mr. Cecil B. Watts with everything he had. And what he didn't have he begged or borrowed or even stole to turn the heat up on the asshole.

And in the end, with the help of some very powerful FBI contacts and friends at the Justice Department and even some of the scumbags he'd put in prison, he'd finally managed to put one very large dent in the previously untouchable world of Cecil Watts

He didn't fully realize it until today, but he'd hurt Watts in the worst possible way: he'd made his own people doubt him. And in the deadly world of drug dealing that usually meant death was lurking just around the corner. Because once the cartels didn't trust you, you were already as good as dead.

"You know, Charlie, there's really no reason why we can't be friends, or at least keep in touch with each other," Watts smiled as he crossed the room.

Sitting down next to his ex-father-in-law, he put one hand on Charlie's knee and went on like they were long time childhood friends.

"I realize at times we haven't exactly seen eye to eye on a lot of things, but I've always respected you, and I'm sure in your own way you've always respected me.

"If for nothing more, at least for being a good provider for your daughter, and for poor little Sara, of course," he quickly added in a smooth, soothing tone.

The man went on and on, speaking to Charlie in that same soothing voice, patting his knee occasionally as he lied about how much more they had in common than just poor little Sara and how they should be supporting each other now through their grief. Her terrible death was probably just meant to happen, he said, and maybe so was the bonding that these two grown men could take from such a horrible experience. He said that even if Charlie went back to L.A. and chose never to come back to this wonderful place where Sara and her mother had been so terribly happy, he would understand, because, he said, he knew all about pain and suffering and being around things that constantly reminded you of dear, departed loved ones.

He said he loved Charlie dearly, as only one man could love another when they'd both suffered such a terrible loss.

Through the whole smooth, well-rehearsed speech, Charlie Custer sat there amid the expensive surroundings and stared silently at the hand rubbing his knee. He could picture that hand beating his own loving wife. Just as he could picture that same hand fondling his own beautiful child. A puffy fat paw that had slammed the door shut on two lives so full of promise.

Finally the monologue ended and Watts moved away, strolling to the bar at the other end of the room to make another drink. Charlie hadn't touched his, and wouldn't, no matter how badly he needed to. From the way Watts strutted away it was obvious he was pleased with his performance.

"So, whatta ya think, pal?" Watts asked and smiled easily to show his perfect teeth.

Charlie Custer mumbled something that couldn’t be heard from the other end of the room, then rose slowly from the expensive leather sofa like a very tired old man who'd seen enough death and enough funerals in his lifetime.

“Huh?” Watts said. “I didn't quite catch what you said, my friend.”

In two astonishingly quick strides Charlie Custer was across the room, the movement shattering the picture of the tired old man seen only seconds earlier.

The first blow, a vicious backhanded slap, sent Watts slamming against the wall. As his head bounced off the expensive wallpaper like a jack-in-the-box clown, a second backhand sent it pounding into it again. One good knee rammed to the balls finished Mr. Cecil B. Watts and left him slumped in a corner. Blood from his face splattered, and then dripped, off the wallpaper and finally found its way onto the expensive Oriental rugs.

“I said you beat and raped my daughter, and when you couldn't get off on that sick shit anymore, you let your dope-dealing friends do the same thing. You fuckin’ bastard! And when Sara got old enough you did the same thing to her, didn’t you?” His voice boomed off the walls with pent up anguish and pure hatred for the man on the floor.

In a response that would only surprise those who didn't truly know him, Cecil Watts smiled. His face lit up greedily as he clutched his balls with one hand and his broken nose with the other and thought about the good old days.

Custer was a cop. Retired or not, he was still a cop with a cop’s pathetic little morals. And even with his hand twitching like a live wire inside his coat to finger-fuck the cannon he never left home without, Watts knew he'd always live by a cop's stupid, simplistic rules. He was as safe as he could be. And he knew it.

“Yeah, daddy-boy, I fucked both them bitches, and then passed them `round plenty to my friends! So fuckin' what? Them nigger bitches are a dime a dozen, man! And I beat on both of `em, too, till their bones were ready to snap, every damn chance I could, `cause, like you said, I needed that kind of thrill to make my big dick hard!” He laughed loudly as he paused a second to let what he’d said sink in, then went on.

“And it got hard, old man! Real fuckin' hard! Sometimes even I couldn't believe how them black bitches with all their pathetic whimpering and whining could get my old dick up and lookin' so good! Hell, with them two, I almost didn't need no Viagra, man. Almost made me feel like a teenager in the back seat of an old Chevy again.

"You remember those days, now don't you, grandpa? Those days when you were nothin' but a slave workin' the plantation for the white man, watchin' the mastr' fuck your mama every night?"

Watts stopped for a moment again to grin broadly at Charlie, laughing loudly as the old man's gun hand seemingly jumped two feet at the mention of the old plantation days. Eventually he continued on, still grinning like the cat that had just eaten the canary. Or at least beaten it up real good.

"But like I said, so fuckin' what?

"Those sluts are dead, man. Dead and stinkin'. And as far as the rest of the world's concerned, it couldn't have happened to two more deserving bitches. They asked for it, daddy-boy...and they got it...real good!

"But you and I, see, we still alive. We still walkin' and talkin' and breathin'. And if you want to keep on this way, then you better just walk away and leave me and my goddamn business alone. You hear me, Charlie-boy? Just walk away..."

Charlie Custer's right hand suddenly stopped stroking the cold metal hanging under his armpit, his mind so filled with hatred he wasn't even aware of the movement stopping as he leaned closer to hear the threat. He wasn't the kind of man who got threatened every day. And on those rare days he did, it usually came down to a real bad ending.

"...if not, then I'll just have to kill that pal of yours, y'know, that blond sufer bum you hang out with in L.A. What's his name, daddy-boy, Jack Irish, or some fuckin'horseshit like that? Come to think of it, now ain't he about the only livin' thing left for you to baby and fret over like a little momma…huh, now ain't he?

"You keep fuckin' with me, nigger, and spreadin' them goddamn rumors and I'll give your goddamn black ass the very real privilege of dragging his sliced up fuckin' ass out of a dumpster too. Exactly, and listen to me closely now, grandpa, I mean exactly like you did with that tasty little bitch Sara."

Charlie's face went blank as Watts eyed him closely, still smiling.

"That's right, daddy-boy! You keep on being real cute and see how much all this fuckin' bullshit costs you!"

Watts' words seemed to pound off every wall of the mansion. In the few seconds of silence that followed it became painfully clear that Charlie wasn't the only one who'd done his homework. Cecil Watts also believed in being thorough, in knowing your enemy as well as you know yourself and keeping him very, very close. In his rush to bring the hammer slamming down on him, he'd probably underestimated the man a little. Not that it mattered much today.

Tomorrow it might. But not today.

Charlie Custer knelt down quietly to come face to face with Cecil Watts, grabbing his fat chin with one hand and jerking the fleshy face close so that they stared into each other's eyes.

"No. No, you won't. You won't go near him and you won't go anywhere near L.A.," he quietly said. There was no ranting, no raving, no hand jerking to his gun. There was simply the calm voice of a man very much in control of himself for the first time since he'd found Sara in that dumpster. A man speaking matter-of-factly, as if what he was now saying was indeed etched in stone.

"Because if you do, I can promise you L.A. will be the very last place you'll ever see. You won't be found in a dumpster. You won't be found in a shallow grave. You just won't ever be seen on the face of this earth again. It won't be a very dramatic death, not anything at all like Sara's," he paused for a moment to stare deeper into Watts' eyes.

"But it will be a very painful one. And a very slow one. I can promise you that.

"And when it's all over, when you're on your knees begging God for mercy to end it, all it will take is one round, right here.

"One round, right here," he repeated in a whisper. He suddenly released the fat chin and pounded a finger dead center into Watts' forehead.

Their eyes locked for a moment longer, and then Charlie got up and turned away. His thoughts about revenge, both his own and Watts', and covering Aaron's ass could wait until he got back on his own turf. It had been a very violent last few minutes. Then again, for the most part, it had been a very violent life. But he also knew precious too little of that violent past had felt as good as these last few seconds.

Wanting to hang onto that feeling just a little longer, Charles Alexander Custer suddenly wheeled and rammed a boot heel into the flesh where his finger had been jabbing.

The Oriental rug was completely ruined in only seconds.

CHAPTER 9

"Hey, Aaron, my friend, long time no see! How ya doin'?
"Good, Franco, I'm doing good. Let me have a beer, okay?"

"Man, your face still bleedin', huh. You want a couple shooters with that?"

"""No, not tonight. Just the beer, okay."

"What? I don't believe what I'm hearin'! No tequila? Well, I be goddamned! Never thought I'd hear that!"

"Yeah, me too."

"Hey, listen, Aaron. I've been readin' 'bout you in one of them magazines, you know, one of them People magazines. Hell, man, I never knew you were in Vietnam, man. And a fuckin' Green Beret! And winnin' the Medal of Honor, well, that's jus' fuckin' incredible, man! Jus' fuckin' incredible, you know. Jus' like fuckin' John Wayne, man…"

"Yeah, yeah, really incredible. Look, just the beer, okay?"

"Yeah, man, sure. I know you vets don't like talkin' 'bout things like that, man, but you should be proud, man. Really proud."

"Yeah."

"Y'know, I saw on TV the other day that broad you saved said she'd fuck you in a heartbeat, no matter what happened to your face. Jus' cause you saved her ass, and all. And she's a real hot lookin' little bitch!"

"Yeah, she is. Hey, look, Franco, you seen Charlie around?

"Custer? No, man. Haven't seen his ass in weeks."

"Well, I'm gonna go check a few other places. Maybe someone's seen him..."

"Don't waste your time, man. I know every joint in this town and every bartender that pours in those shitholes and no one's seen that guy in weeks, man.

"No one."

That conversation, and a dozen others like it replayed over and over in Aaron' head as he sat in another bar, in another country. With another beer.

"Una cervesa, senor?"

"Yeah." Aaron nodded at the waitress. He put the bottle in a neat row along with the eight other empty ones in front of him and watched several fat black cockroaches scurry across the table. He'd been watching the cockroaches for over an hour now as he thought about what his next move should be.

As promised, an envelope - complete with airline tickets, instructions and a whole wad of cash - had mysteriously been slipped under his door three nights after the call from someone using Ricky Simon's name. Aaron was surprised but not exactly stunned. He'd been dealing with reporters for a while now and knew pretty much what was in their dirty little bag of tricks.

So he had a pretty good hunch this guy would follow up on his call.

After racking his brain trying to think of which station or reporter would pull such a stunt, one stood out like a sore thumb. Some idiot from MSMBC was begging him to do what he called "The Unveiling", sort of like an upscale version of what LaBron James had done in his infamous "The Decision", had to be the guy. This fool not only wanted the interview to take place in the very alley that the fight was in, but after reliving the entire thing, complete with juicy comments from the whore he'd rescued, he was supposed to strip away his bandages and show the entire world his fucked-up face. Aaron pointed out, between laughs, that James had taken a lot of heat for his show and his audacity to think that the entire world would give a damn about who he played for next season so why the hell would this be any different. The guy, Johnny Mo, Ace Reporter, as he referred to himself, and always, always in the third person, countered back with James impacted only the world of sports but Aaron's heroic deeds had an effect on every human being on the entire planet. So, of course, this would be viewed in a much more positive light. And he added with emphasis that the planet deserved, no, not only deserved but demanded, to see the price that it cost to protect each other in this crazy world. In this case, that price was his sewn together mug.

And, of course, revealing it to the world would be must see TV!

Like hell it would, Aaron had told the guy, and ended the conversation by telling him to fuck off. But that didn't stop him from calling each and every day and making a fuckin' pest of himself. Aaron had an idea the guy just wouldn't take no for an answer, not with what he thought was such a terrific idea, so he probably dug a little harder, found out that Aaron was working for Custer Investigations when all this shit happened, and uncovered what he probably thought was a little leverage in the name Ricky Simon.

As to why the hell he wanted to meet in the boonies in Mexico, Aaron didn't have the faintest clue.

So after a week of busting his ass looking for Charlie and coming up with zip, he'd used that ticket himself and hopped on the plane and followed the handwritten instructions to the letter. He ended up here, in a shitty little bar so damn far from civilization he wasn't sure he could find his way back without some super-sophisticated GPS device, all set to play a nice little game of cat and mouse with Johnny Mo, dumb-shit reporter. The ace reporter was supposed to meet him right here, third table from the door, at midnight. It was now almost two and so far nothing had happened.

Killing his beer in one swig, Aaron knew he'd bust a gut if he waited any longer to take a piss. Laughing at the thought of pissing his pants as he waited for a big super-secret rendezvous with a man who wanted to make him even more famous, he got up, waved adios to his fat cockroach buddies and weaved towards the head.

The shitter of the bar was much longer than it was wide, making it seem strangely narrow and long, almost like an endless hallway instead of a room. Graffiti-covered plywood and exposed 2 x 4's made up the walls. The toilets were overflowing with crusty shit. And just like at his table, well-fed cockroaches roamed at will. The scent of shit and piss, mixed in with the overpowering smell of vomit, hung in the air like a nasty reminder of just where he was.

A small, dirty peasant, stinking every bit as bad as the room itself, brushed by Aaron as he entered, nodding only slightly as he passed. A second later he heard that man's raspy voice and the door lock at almost the same time. The voice was unmistakable. So were the words.

"Guess I didn't quite make myself clear enough, did I, kid? You wanna tell me what the hell I need to see you for? I told you I needed to see Charlie, didn't I!"

Ricky Simon waited a moment, then spat in disgust.

"Don't give a goddamn rat's ass 'bout you!"

As a stunned Aaron turned to face him, Ricky moved towards him, his left hand hidden under a faded wet green poncho.

"Where the fuck is Charlie?"

Caught completely off guard, Aaron stared back dumbly at the legend he had heard so much about. A legend who was supposedly dead.

A legend who was very much alive.

"I said where the fuck is Charlie, wonder boy?" The tone in his voice quickly switched from disgust to anger. "Either you come up with a real good answer or I'm gonna use this damn thing on you!" His left hand jerked out from underneath the wet poncho. Along with it came a shiny black shotgun.

The unmistakable trademark of Ricky Simon. As unmistakable as the scar on his left cheek.

"Am I makin' myself clear, kid?"

"I...I don't...Christ, man, I looked everywhere..."

Before he could complete the sentence the bathroom door rattled. Softly, almost as if it could have been imagined by both of them.

Ricky whirled to look at the door, then backed slowly away from it as the soft rattle became louder, then exploded into pounding. He continued backing away from the door until he reached the middle of the room.

"Shit, kid, you musta led them right to me! Probably on your goddamn ass right from the plane!" He whispered more to himself than to Aaron as his eyes searched for a way out. "Goddamn useless rookie, I should have never trusted your sorry ass in the first place!

"Tough luck, kid. But you're gonna have to deal with these slick motherfuckers yourself…"

With those words he trained the shotgun at the far wall, nodding at the door and the banging coming from behind it.

"You dug your own goddamn grave, kid," he winked. "I got my way out!"

In an instant the wall was completely gone. And so was Ricky Simon.

Instinctively turning away to shield himself from the debris and smoke from the explosion that seemingly torn the roof off the bar, Aaron ran into a fist. Several more blows, all pounded into the white gauze on the left side of his face, sent him staggering to the floor. Crumpled up and helpless, Aaron noticed, almost as if dreaming, that the door that had been rattling so innocently just a few seconds earlier, now, like the far wall, was also completely gone.

"How much did he tell you?"

No introductions, no explanations, no phony stories. Just a few jabs into the shitter door, then a few more into the white gauze and then a simple question.

Rolled up into a tiny ball by the pain tearing through his face, Aaron struggled to make sense out of what had just happened. Ricky Simon was alive but now gone, that much he was sure of. This other guy, the one with the question, the one that had just kicked his ass with some karate-type bullshit, must have been the one who kicked down the door. And the same one Ricky was running from. Somehow that seemed to connect the dots, for the moment, anyway, so Aaron tried to raise his head up a little to sneak a peek at the man now walking back towards him through the smoke after briefly inspecting the wall Ricky'd blown away.

The man was Vietnamese, that much Aaron was sure of. Even with only one eye working, he couldn't miss that. Not the scrawny little VC type, either. Hell no. This guy was one of the much bigger, beefier Chinese-bred assholes that came complete with packs and helmets and an unlimited supply of ammo. The kind that called themselves NVA regulars. The same kind that had pounded on Aaron's body once before.

The memory of that first pounding made him feel like puking. So did the fact that this guy wore a double-breasted silk suit, along with shiny new wingtips, and reeked like a fuckin' whore of Pierre Cardin.

Only now, crumpled on the floor like a bleeding puppet, did Aaron realize how incredibly stupid he'd been.

Ricky's instructions had warned about keeping an eye out for anyone who looked suspicious, out of place, out of whack.

Anyone who just plain didn't belong.

Because chances were good, he said, very good, that he just might be followed down here or possibly pick up a tail once the plane landed. He didn't bother to say who would do the tailing, or why. But then again, he was expecting Charlie, so maybe no explanation was needed.

In a filthy little bar jammed full with Mexican peasants wearing nothing fancier than sandals, jeans and baseball caps, this gook asshole with the silk suit stuck out like a sore thumb.

And Aaron Ireland hadn't been able to spot him.

Charlie Custer would have with ease. But the boy wonder with the pocket full of press clippings didn't have the faintest clue who or what looked out of place, even in a shithole like this.

And it didn't take a genius to figure out he was going to pay a big price for that sorry-ass incompetence.

He didn't have a clue what this guy wanted. But he knew if someone like Ricky Simon was running from him, then he had to be bad-ass. And that calm, utterly professional just-another-day-at-the-office tone in his voice did nothing to change that impression. Aaron didn't doubt he'd kill with that same calmness when the time came, either.

Reaching Aaron, the man smiled, almost out of pity, at the lump of shit curled up on the floor.

"I'll only ask one more time. There is an easy way to do this, and then, there is always the hard way. You and I both know you'll never leave this room alive, so for your own sake, why not just take the easy way and I promise to spare you as much pain as possible, ok?

"Now, how much did he tell you?" He spoke in textbook English without slurring or rounding off his words. Hanoi and rice paddies obviously were a long, long way in his past.

Aaron nodded weakly in agreement and looked slowly around at the smoke-filled room, at the black and white checkered floor soaked in his blood, at the far wall that was now nothing more than a few splinters courtesy of a long gone Ricky Simon, at the fat cockroaches crawling around the toilets completely oblivious to his pain, and finally back at the NVA regular standing in front of him. And couldn't think of anything to say that wouldn't get his ass kicked real good again. And then killed.

"He didn't tell me nothin', ok? I don't know nothin' about nothin'. All I know is that when someone started pounding on the door," he paused and nodded at where the bathroom door should have been, "He just went completely nuts and pulls out a goddamn shotgun from out of nowhere and then just stands there and blows the whole fuckin' wall away. And then he just walks away...

"And that's all I know, I swear. He said nothin'. Christ, like I said, he pulled the trigger and just walked away like a goddamn ghost!" The panic in Aaron's voice filled the room as he raised the palms of his hands upward. The simple gesture looked like one of total surrender.

"Ricky Simon always seems to vanish like a ghost, doesn't he?" the other man replied quietly, more to himself than to Aaron.

Suddenly spinning away from Aaron, the man walked towards the burned-out wall to inspect it again. Even his silk suit and perfect English couldn't hide his contempt for Aaron. He wanted to kill him right now. The longer he watched him crawling on the floor like one of those disgusting cockroaches crawling around the toilets, the more he listened to his desperate voice whimpering pathetic lies, the more he had to fight the almost overwhelming urge to plant the gun squarely in his mouth and squeeze off a round.

But he had his orders. And they would be followed. He'd been instructed to get answers first, then quietly dispose of the body.

So far, to his surprise, the guy had held up better physically than expected. At least he was still conscious. And somewhat quiet, considering the pain he must be in. He'd been advised to work his face over good, and he had. He'd worked it over so well that blood practically poured from those old alley wounds. And yet the guy was still lying to him. It had actually surprised him how easily the stitches tore away from the flesh. You could actually see the ugly wounds opening up again, as if coming to life, and almost breathing through the dripping gauze. He'd never seen anything quite like it before. They looked painful as hell. And he knew they must hurt like a bitch.

And yet the guy was still lying to him.

Round Two would be different. He'd make damn sure of that. He'd hammer away, this time with the metal butt of his 9mm, at that face with the one eye swollen shut and the dripping gauze until the gun's butt went clean through to the other side of his stupid, brainless skull, if that's what it took.

He had his orders. And if he didn't get the truth from this idiot, then he'd probably wind up in the same place that this guy was headed for in the next five minutes.

And he had absolutely no intention of dying.

Whirling around to face his prisoner, he silently reminded himself to hold his own personal desires in check, at least until he had answers. As he did he straightened his red power tie with his left hand in an almost automatic gesture. With his right hand he slowly pulled out his 9mm from inside his silk coat, twirling the gun on his index finger so that the metal butt faced Aaron, and smiled in anticipation. The question came a few seconds later.

"How much did he tell you?"

He smiled again for a moment, then began the short walk back to Aaron.

"Believe me, I'm going to enjoy this more than I could ever tell you..."

As he spoke, two shotgun barrels slipped quietly through the wreckage that had been the far wall. With his back to that wall, both barrels inched forward unnoticed by the man in the silk suit. Aaron didn't notice them either. His one good eye was trained solely on the gun's butt and the pain that piece of metal would soon be delivering.

In the tiny enclosed room the incoming blasts of the shotgun sounded more like the roar of a battleship's cannon than that of a hand held weapon. The remaining plywood walls and 2 x 4's shuddered and seemingly rose off the ground with each blast as smoke instantly choked the room again. Along with the smoke came the sickening odor of burnt flesh.

And the stench of death.

The first blast ripped through the Viet squarely in the back. The force of the almost point blank hit sent him slamming towards the opposite wall the instant the pellets touched flesh. The second blast practically cemented what was left of his body to it.

Aaron was blown against the same wall by both blasts, and by the body driven past him. Dumbfounded, he wasn't sure if he was dead or alive until the smell of burnt flesh forced its way up his nose. Then he just lay very still and prayed for the best.

It didn't take long before the dirty little man with the big black shotgun came for him.

"I tried to tell ya, kid, you and Charlie got yourselves into a world of hurt! And now I'm up to my goddamn ass in it too!" Ricky Simon said. His voice was very low, barely above a whisper, and calm. Even through all thc smoke and all the splintered plywood and all the roasted flesh, he still seemed to be chastising Aaron like a teacher would with an unruly student.

"Am I makin' myself clear, kid? Huh? Goddamnit, am I finally makin' myself clear?"

Aaron didn't understand a single word Ricky Simon was saying. He could care less if the words made sense or not. He only knew that the hand reaching down thought the smoke and pulling him away from that mangled body next to him had saved his life. And for now that was more than enough.

As Aaron was being dragged away into the rainy night and the freedom it held, he looked back only once at the tiny shitter, and at the body that was jammed awkwardly between one of the toilets and the wall, staring for just a moment at the shiny new wingtips now soaking in red.

CHAPTER 10

The sweetness of a woman's scent surrounded him, forcing Aaron into the present. A present that seemed every bit as violent as his past. He'd been thinking about Vietnam again. Ever since Ricky had dropped him off and he'd dashed straight to the hotel bar and started drinking, he'd been thinking about nothing but napalm strikes and body bags.

And the dripping red wingtips of a dead man.

But the woman's questions finally were driving him insane. She sat on the low-backed bar stool near the end of the bar looking every bit like the flaming red-haired whore she was. Her short, tight skirt clung to her body to expose thighs barely covered by stocking tops and the tips of a garter belt. With every movement the skirt would inch up higher to show off more of the white flesh between the top of the old fashioned nylons and her hemline. One red stiletto pump dangled from the toes of her crossed right leg. Surprisingly, her face, with the hollow, high-cheekbone look of a model, was tastefully done. The only excess was lipstick, which nonetheless looked absolutely perfect on her. Any other time, any other day - or maybe with just more booze - and Aaron wouldn't have given a damn about what was coming out of those perfect red lips.

But today her thousand and one questions were driving him up the goddamn wall.

He'd put up with a battered, swollen face. And he'd deal with temporarily having only one eye to work with. Hell, he'd even live with a throbbing left hand, courtesy of too goddamn many of Ricky's stray shotgun pellets. Booze, lots of booze, would take the edge off the pain. And hopefully dull some of the memories.

But he couldn't put up with any more of her questions. At least not until the sea of tequila he'd inhaled began to have the desired effect.

The very slutty June Jones had teetered into Aaron's world on spiked heels and tight silk skirts the day he'd gotten out of Intensive Care. But she wasn't just another private dick groupie looking to sneak into his room with the hopes of fucking the new hero into another coma. Hell no! Instead she stormed in like the goddamn Gestapo, spitting profanities, throwing magazines with his face adorning the cover at him and bitching to the entire world that the boy wonder had righteously screwed up by catching the wrong guy.

But god, was she a looker. Coming across at times like an educated, refined model, and then reverting in the blink of an eye to a dirty little street slut, the combination, like the look, was awesome. And completely irresistible. Even when all she could do was rant and rave and curse and swear and sometimes even pout like a spoiled child about what an incompetent little punk he was for catching the wrong guy, all Aaron could think about was getting into her pants. And then pumping that dirty little mouth for all it was worth.

And, oh yeah, along with all her non-stop shouting about his incompetence as a detective, she also couldn't shut up about knowing who the real killer was, either.

Supposedly, one of the whores killed earlier was a real close friend of hers, and she vowed like an angel of revenge to scour the earth until she tracked down the bastard and made him pay for his sins. That's what she claimed. Aaron had his doubts. Not about the revenge part, something told him she definitely had the guts for that. He doubted the real close friends' part. She just didn't seem to be the kind of person who really gave a damn about anyone but herself, even when she was fucking him to death. So why waste your precious self on someone else's murder? Anyway, after completing her own supposedly thorough investigation, she now had the field narrowed down to one bad guy. And only one.

The trouble was, once Aaron heard the guy's name, he couldn't help but bust a gut laughing. Jesus Christ, the guy was so damn far down the list of suspects that no one had even bothered talking to him, including the cops. He'd heard about him, yeah. Everybody knew who Jackie B. was. But talking to him would have been as big a waste of his time as talking to her was most days.

All his laughter got him was another round of salty insults from the woman along with the solemn vow to make him pay for doubting her.

Despite the rough beginning, the woman had hung around. That was over a month ago. She didn't give a damn about Aaron and Christine or what they might have had. She was here now, the other woman wasn't, and that, simply was enough said about that.

Aaron didn't mind her hanging around, especially when he'd been drinking hard. But he was also smart enough to know she stuck around only in the hopes of somehow convincing him that Jack Burnfin, or Jackie B. as everyone called him, was the real killer. Christ, she just couldn't seem to get that poor bastard out of her crosshairs. And didn't give a damn that someone else, with a full confession signed, sealed and delivered, was already behind bars for the murders. She didn't give a damn either that the killings in Hollywood had stopped - no more carved up bodies, no more missing ring fingers, no more black robes and garbage dumpsters.

The lady didn't give a shit about any of that. She was simply totally convinced that good old Jackie B. was behind it all. And that the killing would start up again. Very soon and, if possible, even nastier than before. If that were possible.

Aaron laughed at her fortune-telling abilities and didn't buy any of it. Not one single profane word that came out of those perfect red lips. But they kind of settled on the unspoken agreement that if he listened to her cockeyed theories every once in a while, and maybe even checked out a few of her crazy leads, then he would also be free to fuck her brains out every single night if he wanted to.

And with this woman he wanted to. A lot.

The woman was a slut. There was never any doubt about that. She dressed like a slut. She talked like a slut. She even wiggled down the street like a slut. She had the whole sweet ball bustin' package. And Aaron loved the whole damn show.

She wasn't the one he was in love with, there was never any doubt about that. But with Christine giving him his walking papers, this woman would definitely do. And besides, she looked at him, bandages and all, not through him, and treated him like what happened to his face didn't matter. Christine never had the chance to pass that test and now he'd never really know what part his mangled face played in her decision to walk away, if any. So what the hell, any port in a storm, right?

And he'd seen a lot worse in this old world than the wonderfully slutty Ms. June Jones.

But today, right now, at ten in the morning in the swank bar of a very swank five-star hotel, Ms. June Jones was driving him crazy with a thousand-and-one questions about things she couldn't possibly know anything about. He knew Ricky Simon and his murderous past had never come up before with her. And while she had at times pressed him for details about Charlie and his work, drunk or not, he'd always managed to keep Charlie out of her line of fire by saying very little about his friend. Yet here she was acting like some kind of goddamn expert about both of them.

"Are you absolutely certain this Ricky guy didn't tell you anything, Aaron? I mean, he must have said something, baby, and whatever it was, someone must have thought it was pretty goddamn important, right?" she smiled. With that said, she laced her fingers behind her head and leaned back in the barstool to further expose black garter belts taunt and straining. Aaron didn't notice the indentations they made in the soft skin of her thighs because his eyes never strayed from his shot glass.

"I mean, people just don't go around chasing after other people and then getting themselves killed in the process if it isn't about something pretty goddamn important, right?

"Are you absolutely, positively certain Ricky didn't say anything to you? I mean, we all know how much Ricky likes to brag and bullshit and carry on about all the important shit he knows, right? Are you sure he didn't say even the tiniest little thing to you about why he was there?

"Or maybe he mentioned something about your pal Charlie and what he was working on before he disappeared, huh, baby?"

Instead of answering, Aaron sat silently and drank, one shot following another as he winced at her stupid questions.

"Well, maybe it'll come to you later. I mean, big, bad combat veteran and all, you've still been through such a terrible ordeal with last night and all. Maybe after all this has calmed down a little, you'll be able to remember better about what you two guys talked about."

After offering her final piece of advice, the woman leaned forward on her barstool and began downing shooters too. Recrossing her legs, the smooth nylons hissing softly as they rubbed against each other, she didn't bother pulling her skirt down to stop exposing all she had to anyone who passed by. But she did shut up.

Aaron noticed the silence, and thanked God for it. Out of the corner of his one good eye he also noticed the slow, tantalizing way her lips worked over the lemon slices that automatically followed every shot.

The silence ended too soon with her third shot.

"But, y'know what, baby, maybe this whole thing was just about money. Maybe Ricky just owed that poor Oriental guy a lot of money, maybe a whole shitload of money, and when Charlie didn't show up he killed him instead of paying him off. That kind of makes sense, doesn't it? I mean, he probably needed to borrow the money from Charlie…and no Charlie means no money…so he jus' kills the guy instead!" she smiled and spread her hands out in a questioning gesture, her skirt sliding even higher up as she moved.

"And maybe that's why he was so hot to have your buddy Charlie meet him down here. Maybe he just wanted to borrow some cash from him. Or maybe he figured that with your friend Charlie being such a hot shit detective and all, that maybe he wouldn't mind helping him kill this Oriental guy instead of paying him.

"Yeah, y'know, that makes perfect sense. Maybe this whole goddamn thing was about money! Plain and simple as that!"

Aaron remained quiet, still drinking as he thought about what she'd just said. He was finally drunk, or damn close to getting there. But even drunk, he knew Ricky's troubles had nothing to do with money. Hell, as they'd run down that alley from the shitter and ducked into a taxi Ricky had stashed there, he'd seen Ricky toss the driver a wad of bills that looked like nothing but hundreds, then shouted instructions in Spanish and they'd taken off like a fuckin' rocket.

No, Ricky Simon didn't have money problems.

But he was drunk. And the long nyloned legs in front of him were finally getting his attention. And so was the parade of men strolling slowly by and eating her alive with their eyes and him knowing that, out of all of them, rich or poor, handsome or disfigured, she'd be only with him tonight. Fucking him hard and nasty. And besides, he was damned tired of seeing those lucky lemon slices hogging all the action from those pouting red lips. It was time to put them to work on something just a little bit meaner. And a whole lot harder.

"You're right. It's probably just about money. Money, money and more damn money," he lied, and smiled for the first time since he'd raced into the bar. Then he slid his good hand past her now uncrossed open legs and began fumbling away at the exposed white panties that always seemed to be peeking out.

The rain beat down on them, drowning everything and making the simple act of seeing almost impossible. The two boys stared into that rain, looking across from their hiding place in the dense jungle across a narrow river to where a small trail began on the other side.

The trail began on the muddy river bank and then snaked its' way into the jungle before being completely swallowed up after only ten feet. It looked quiet and innocent enough, but both of them knew what lay ahead on the parts of that narrow path they couldn't see.

"Man, that's a fuckin' ambush jus' waitin' to happen. Fuckin' gooks be all over that goddanm trail tonight...", the taller one whispered. "C'mon man, let's diddi, fuck, we've already gone further than the Capt'n said we hadda, right?'

The other one, seeing the same thing his friend did, nodded at his partner shivering in the rain. He knew his shaking had nothing to do with the weather. He couldn't remember when his friend had lost it, but all hope that they might somehow get out of this shit alive didn't exist in his soul anymore.

Maybe it was the constant running and fighting, the ambushes and the dead they left behind, of the last few days that had left their company a battered mess, but somewhere Walter Russell had lost it. All it took was one look in his lifeless eyes to know that.

"Man, let's fuckin' diddi..."

"You know your mamma's gonna kill you for that chicken-scratch shit," Aaron smiled as he pointed at the other's right arm in the hopes of pumping some life into his friend.

Russell looked down at his proud prize from a stoned R and R they'd taken only a few weeks ago; a large red, white and blue Playboy bunny dancing above big, black letters-USMC. Running his hand over the rain-slickened bunny, he finally smiled.

"Yeah, man, that was one fuckin' good time, huh? Jus' like everybody sayin', Bangkok is one fuckin' fine place to be! And don't go bullshittin' me, brother, I know you wish you'd gotten one too!"

Aaron shook his head. He liked the way the bunny looked, especially the way it seemed to dance whenever Russell flexed his bicep, but not nearly enough to have one etched on his own flesh.

His friend's smiled quickly faded as his gaze returned to the path on the other side of the river.

"Man, let's fuckin' diddi...I'd rather have my momma rant and rave at me like a goddamn preacher man for this here bunny every day for the rest of my life than walk down that fuckin' trail..."

"Yeah, okay," Aaron nodded. "Let's go tell the Capt'n he needs to find another way out, 'cause this motherfucker definitely ain't the way..."

With those words the jungle seemed to come to life around them, as if hearing their words about a possible escape route awoke something.

"Yeah, man, let's fuckin' diddi...real fuckin'quick!" Aaron whispered, then slipped back into the lush jungle for cover on the way home.

Aaron bolted up in bed, the sheets around him drenched in sweat. The booze had finally worn off. And now his face hurt like a son-of-a-bitch. So did his wounded left paw. Next to him, the woman slept like the proverbial baby, oblivious to everything.

He'd been dreaming about Vietnam again. More to the point, about his last few days there. He must have thrashed around like some kind of wounded animal, because there were thin streaks of blood running down from the wall above the bed's headboard. They had dried badly and probably ruined the hotel's chic wallpaper.

And all that hadn't budged the woman next to him. Not that he really gave a damn if she was awake or not. Most nights, after waking up from a drinking binge with her, the last thing he wanted was to have to deal with her and her mouth.

Yeah, him and Ms. Jones had gotten into a pretty regular routine of drinking until they crawled away from whatever bar they ended up at and then fucking their little brains out. He used her, she used him. And when it was over all he wanted was for her to pack her shit and go off to wherever it was she called home.

It was pretty obvious, maybe even a little comical if you took the time to really think about it, but sex, booze, and dead whores were about the only things they had in common. Or even talked about, for that matter. Hell, he couldn't remember a single time when they hadn't been drinking hard, fucking hard and arguing hard about Jackie B.

He knew he felt different about her and her non-stop mouth when he was sober. But he also knew he hadn't been that way for a while now.

After a few moments of promising himself that he was definitely swearing off the booze, and then looking at the woman sleeping peacefully next to him and shaking his head, Aaron limped out of bedroom. He must have slept six or seven hours, but he still had that boozy feeling as he wandered around the suite sucking up coffee until he eventually ended up on the balcony. Shivering in the cold, he counted himself lucky he'd only thrown up once so far. And hadn't stumbled over any of the furniture, yet.

Looking out at the mountains in the distance that were partially hidden in fog, Aaron thought about the last month and how he wished none of it had ever happened. Prayed that none of it had ever happened. A moment later all his thoughts about heroic rescues and their consequences vanished as he began to realize something about those mountains looked familiar to him. And the longer he stared at them, strangely enough, the clearer and more recognizable they became. Until they became so familiar it hurt. He could see the medi-vac choppers circling those hillsides, hovering low to pick up the wounded and dead, his ears ringing with the sharp crack of AK-47 fire raising up to meet them. He knew those goddamn mountains like the back of his hand. He should. He'd humped every one of them before - in Vietnam.

There was the Rockpile. And the mountains around Khe Sanh. And Con Thien. And the smaller one on his right was Hill 881 where he'd lost most of his friends in only a few days.

And all of them, every single goddamn one of them, were right here, all these years later, staring back at him through the Mexican fog as if they recognized him too.

Sadly, the thought finally seeped through that everything in his life lately had been about Vietnam. Not just the gook who'd been wasted in the shitter. And not just the beating he'd taken in that alley. But everything. Every single damn thing.

And that included the dreams he'd been having.

From a rainy Hollywood alley to a dirty Mexican shitter, with steps for a thousand ugly memories in between, his whole life, especially the violence that had passed through it the last month, had been about Vietnam. He only now had the guts to face up to it.

And now that it was time to face the music, he had to admit he even found himself thinking about his first kill again. A little killing that was easily as ugly as his torn up face.

They'd limped down from one of those mountains he seemed to see so clearly now, bleeding from another ass kicking. Aaron was on point and saw him first. From the moment their eyes met, and the kid waved at him, Aaron knew he wasn't a part of any of this. He was just a scrawny little kid playing in the rain with a half-starved dog at his side.

He pulled the trigger anyway. He even took pleasure in the perfect automatic stitch drilled in the kid's chest. And just to prove what a truly tough bastard he was, even before the kid spit up his last breath, Aaron had already whipped out his K-bar and begun carving on his forehead. The initials A.I. came first, followed by M\3\7 - Aaron Ireland, Mike Company, 3rd Battalion, 7th Marine Regiment. Fuck no, he wasn't the kind of man to settle for the small-time bullshit of cutting off ears. No sir, L/Cpl Aaron Ireland, USMC, was only happy after branding the kid with his own personal mark.

And now Aaron Ireland took that mark, too. He may have gotten it in the line of duty while doing a noble deed and it may have come from a straight-edged razor and not a Marine K-bar, but it was still the same mark. Hidden in white hospital gauze or not, it was there all the same. And always would be, no matter what the medical men with all their miracles promised.

Only a fool wouldn't see the sweet irony that in taking an innocent life, and then in saving one years later, that that mark had still found a way to end up on his own flesh.

Maybe he should have expected it. Because he'd swear on his own grave he'd seen that kid on the streets of Hollywood with him just before he'd ducked into the alley that night. The kid was a block away, still smiling, still waving. He didn't have the damn dog with him, but it was the same kid. And in the operating room as they'd stitched his face back together, he didn't think of glory or fame or that he'd somehow saved a life. All he could think about was his own ugly straight edged razor digging into that little gook's forehead.

The boy wonder doing it all over again. Almost as if no time had passed at all.

Yeah, in a clear light, it was more than a little obvious he definitely had a little problem with Vietnam these days.

And in one more true confession, in one more sweet fuckin' irony that only a fool could miss, even the woman he was pining away for was a gook. Christine Ito was half Japanese and bright and brilliant and funny and sexy and long and lean and athletic and adored children and puppies and practically anything else that breathed, especially Calvin the sheepdog, but she was also a gook. And in his world even half slanted eyes made you a gook full time.

Fuck yeah he had a little problem. Almost to the point where it seemed like his whole miserable little world had been boiled down to nothing but Vietnam. To the point where he could look out from the terrace of a swanky hotel smack dab in the middle of South America and pick out the mountains where his friends had died. And where he had killed without thinking twice about it.

And truly believe in what he was seeing.

He had to be going insane. An ugly thought that stayed uncomfortably close to him these days. Because there was just no other goddamn explanation for any of it. Putting his coffee cup down, Aaron Ireland reached for the half-empty tequila bottle on the balcony table.

And started all over again.

CHAPTER 11

"Kid, you in there? Hey kid, that you?" Ricky whispered, staring ahead through the blackness at where he could have sworn something had moved only seconds earlier. He couldn't be sure but he sure thought that looked like movement to him.

He was in an old abandoned cantina, just inside the doorway, on the far outskirts of a small town which was on the far outskirts of just about anywhere civilized. Ricky knew this remote area like the back of his hand from his drug runnin' days and had paid one of his contacts well, very well - hell, he'd probably funded his entire goddamn retirement with what he coughed over to him - to deliver a message to Aaron at his swanky digs a couple hundred miles to the north.

The message was short and sweet: meet him here at the cantina, bring along some travellin' clothes and don't be followed. The plan was to tell the poor bastard just what kinda shit he'stepped into, and then very quietly slip away. If the kid wanted to tag along, fine, if not, then he was on his own. There wasn't much doubt anymore about Charlie's fate. But he felt he owed it to the kid to try and save his sorry ass, if only to repay Custer at least a little. That's if the dumbshit wanted saving at all. If he didn't, then fuck him all to hell, he could join Charlie at the Pearly Gates.

"Kid, that you? C'mon, man, we don't have a lotta time here, know what I mean?" he whispered again.

Moving forward, Ricky quietly pulled the black shotgun out from under his poncho. There was definitely someone up ahead, someone who appeared to be crouching in the doorway that lead to the bar area that a decade ago was always packed with tourists and locals on a Friday night looking for good times and the good drugs that went with it.

It could only be the kid, Ricky thought, smiling to himself. Hell, the dumb son-of-a-bitch was so scared in the shitter two days ago that he was still probably changing his panties every five minutes. And probably crouching in doorways and jumping like a fuckin' jackrabbit when anyone said "boo".

Yeah, Ricky grinned, he definitely looked like the kind of sissy who wore silk boxers.

"Don't shit them panties jus' yet, kid, it's only me…"

The sound of automatic weapon fire, opening up all around him, cut off his last words, splintering the floor and walls where Ricky Simon had been grinning only seconds earlier. A single shotgun blast was heard mixed in with those automatic weapons, overwhelmed by the fire power raking it, before the cantina was once again dark and silent.

CHAPTER 12

Ricky Simon was a dead man. Aaron was as positive of that as he was that he was now jetting it back comfortably to L.A. on Ricky Simon's ticket.

Sitting there in first class surrounded by innocent, well-dressed tourists talking loudly about their own Mexican adventures, Aaron began to get the uneasy feeling that maybe he had something to do with the man's death. Maybe a helluva lot more than he wanted to admit to. Maybe if he hadn't used the ticket meant for Charlie and hadn't shown up in this rathole thinking it was all just a stupid game meant to scare the shit out of some dumb-ass reporter or maybe if he'd been just at least half-assed good at what he was doing and had managed to dig up Charlie in the first place, then maybe none of this would have happened.

And maybe Ricky would still be alive.

Or maybe if he'd only been able to do something as goddamned simple as pick out a Vietnamese killer in a silk suit in a bar full of nothing more than Mexican trash.

But he hadn't been able to do any of that. And Ricky was dead because of it. Even in only knowing the guy ten seconds, Aaron knew the end had to have been ugly and violent.

"Baby, you thinking about that Ricky guy again?" the women's voice sweetly, almost gently, interrupted his thoughts, her hand reaching for his.

"My god, you hung around that damn hotel room for three days waiting for nothing, honey. I just don't know what more you could have done."

Aaron nodded at what she said. He had hung around the hotel for days waiting for some sort of contact from Ricky. A call, a note- hell, even a goddamn thunder bolt from the sky would have been nice- any kind of contact to set up a meeting at a safe place where he would finally explain just what the hell was going on and why his and Charlie's names were on some sort of list.

That contact never came, and on day three Aaron knew the man Charlie Custer always bragged had more balls than any man alive was dead. Brass balls lopped off and left to dry in the sun. Dead for real this time. And along with his death went all his would be explanations.

"I'm sure Ricky's just fine. Like I said all along, baby, this was just about money. Money and not a damn thing more. Ricky's probably just pissed off because you didn't bring Charlie along to bail him out with his money…and now he's gone back into hiding after killin' that guy!"

Then she squeezed Aaron's hand hard to emphasize her point about Ricky Simon being completely broke and simply wanting nothing more that money from Charlie. A point she'd hammered on endlessly during the last three days.

Aaron looked at the perfectly manicured hand holding his, at the long, slender fingers topped off with perfect nails painted red. Outside of her outbursts about what she was just thoroughly positive Ricky had really wanted, she had been strangely quiet lately. Even her usual gutter mouth had been put on hold.

A second later Aaron broke into a soft laugh, grinning at the way a tired mind plays tricks on you. Jesus Christ, he had definitely been hanging around Charlie too damn long because now even he was beginning to do the exact thing that drove him nuts when Charlie did it: question every fuckin'one and every fuckin'thing around you until you had answers that made sense to you. He had almost, almost, mind you, begun to think that the lovely and terrifically slutty Ms. June Jones actually had something to do with Ricky's death.

"What' so funny?"

"Nothing. Nothing at all. I'm just really looking forward to getting home, I guess" Aaron exhaled deeply.

"I know what you mean, baby. Believe me, I know exactly what you mean."

"My God, they killed him! They killed him! Those damned White Devils killed him dead! Oh, God, why? Why him?" an anguished woman's voice, southern and obviously black, cried out from somewhere near the back of the plane.

Aaron's head, as well as every other passenger's in first class, jerked up instantly at the sound of those words, the thought of another terrorist attack thirty thousand feet up stunning everyone into silence. A stunning, tall blond flight attendant, followed by two male attendants, moved cautiously down the aisle towards the coach section where the commotion was. The voice was silent now, with only a muffled weeping echoing through the plane along with the quiet sounds of comforting voices.

A moment later an obviously relieved flight attendant parted the curtains and stepped back into the first class area, taking a deep, refreshing breath as she did.. She had a look of amusement on her face and shook her head almost in disbelief as she addressed the first class passengers.

"Everything's fine folks, just fine...believe me, there's nothing to worry about. It seems that one of our passengers in coach just found out that...what was that again, Bobby?" she stopped, still shaking her head, to glance at one of the male attendants who had followed her into the coach section.

"A basketball player..."

"Oh, yeah, some sort of basketball player had been murdered in Los Angeles a few days ago…"

"A basketball who was a goddamn terrorists!" a voice broke in from the seats in front of Aaron. "A goddamn al-Quaida bomber living right here in our own backyard!"

"Yeah, I heard that, too!" Another voice shouted. "The bastard was an animal! A fuckin' aninal! There's no telling' how many Americans he killed with all his blood money! Whoever killed him should get a goddamn medal or something'!"

"Goddamn right!" a third voice chipped in. "I'd waste the black bastard myself if he wasn't already dead!"

"They outta bury his black ass in Iraq along with the rest of his al-Qaeda buddies!" a female voice shouted above the others as a well-dressed woman stood up and pointed an accusing finger back at third class. "My husband was killed in Iraq two years ago fightin' these animals and left me a widow with four kids to support! And now they're gettin' help from some nigger assholes livin' right here? I can't believe what these goddamned niggers have turned this country into! I say fuck you and fuck every fuckin' al-Qaeda piece of shit!

The woman's bitter outburst and the word "nigger" brought the passenger's uproar to a sudden halt. It was almost as if the woman had spoken what was really on all their minds.

Breaking the momentary silence, the flight attendant continued on, just as she had been trained, trying to quiet the situation as she politely ignored what had just been said.

"Well, apparently this player had been one of the passenger's favorites...I guess..." her words tailed off.

She rebounded gallantly a second later.

"Cocktail anyone, they're on the house, compliments of the Captain!" she cheerily announced.

Aaron watched the stunning attendant, followed obediently by the two male attendants, as she hustled by him with the drink cart. He kept thinking about the voice from the rear of the plane and the words she had cried.

"My God, they killed him!"

Wasn't that what they said when JFK was killed? Or was it Bobby? Or maybe it was when Martin Luther King was murdered? Those strong words were cried with such unbelievably powerful passion and pain over the tragic deaths of truly great men.

And now those very same words were cried over a common athletic. A basketball player. And a terrorists, if what the others said was true. Athletics as gods? And as mad bombers? What kind of sick world have we turned into? Aaron thought, shaking his head.

Maybe it wasn't such a great place to be going home to after all.

He leaned over to say a few words to June Jones about this, but she was too deeply engrossed in her Cosmo to even notice him. Hell, he doubted she was even aware of the sudden eruption of raw passion that had just taken place around them.

Yeah, it really was a helluva world to be going back to.